# MIGHTY TRUCK

WRITTEN BY
**CHRIS BARTON**

ILLUSTRATED BY
**TROY CUMMINGS**

**HARPER**
*An Imprint of HarperCollinsPublishers*

For Owen—C.B.

To Harvey: Thanks for playing cars and trucks
with me while I worked on this book!—T.C.

Mighty Truck
Copyright © 2016
by HarperCollins Publishers
All rights reserved.
Manufactured in China.
No part of this book may be used or reproduced in any
manner whatsoever without written permission except
in the case of brief quotations embodied in critical articles and reviews. For
information address HarperCollins Children's Books,
a division of HarperCollins Publishers,
195 Broadway, New York, NY 10007.
www.harpercollinschildrens.com

ISBN 978-0-06-234478-6

The artist used Adobe Photoshop to create the
digital illustrations for this book.
Typography by Joe Merkel
❖
16 17 18 19 20  SCP  10 9 8 7 6 5 4 3 2 1

First Edition

Everything Clarence did for fun . . .
somehow seemed to get him dirty.

Not just a little splatter-on-the-mud-flaps dirty.
*Really* dirty.
# REALLY WHEELY DIRTY.

MAIN **MT** TRANSPORT

Clarence didn't mind.

But his boss did.

"Clarence, is that you under all that muck?"
Hattie teased. "Clean up before work starts."

"Bruno and I were hoping to have time for donuts," Clarence said. "Won't the rain get me clean?"

"Three cloudbursts, two downpours, and a serious drencher wouldn't do it. Get yourself to a truck wash—now!"

"All right, I'll go." Clarence sighed. "If you say so."

By the time Clarence made it to the truck wash,
thunder was rumbling.

TRUCK
WASH

IN

Suds sprayed.

Slappers whapped.

Water splashed
from every angle.

Just then . . .

Lightning struck. Everything shook. The fizzing, frothing, glowing foam washed Clarence clean. His paint shimmered, glimmered, glistened, and gleamed.

Clarence felt revved up, raring to roll....

"And powerful," he said.

# "REALLY WHEELY POWERFUL."

Soon Clarence found Bruno stuck in some mud.
"Need a little help?"

"No need to dirty yourself, shiny-clean stranger," said Bruno. "My friend Clarence is on his way. We're going for donuts. He'll push me loose."

"You joker," said Clarence.
"All right! Let's go!"
   He meant to give just a
nudge, but . . .

BONK!

"Wow! What
do you know?"

**HELP!**

Donuts would have to wait. Clarence hurried off and found his neighbor Mr. Dent.

He shifted down into his Mighty Truck voice. "What's the trouble, sir?"

"Dude, my cat, Throttle, is stuck in a tree."

"I'll get him down," said Clarence. "Um, where's the tree?"

"It, like, just got hauled away!" Mr. Dent said.

The spade truck had a head start,
but it didn't have mighty speed.
When Clarence caught up,
Throttle was barely hanging on.

Clarence spun
into reverse . . .

Throttle leaped
into his truck bed . . .
and they both headed home.

"Major thanks, dude!" said Mr. Dent.
"Catch you later, uh . . ."
"Just call me Mighty Truck."
Clarence drove away to look for Bruno,
wondering if there was still time for donuts.

Right then, the voice of
Stella the News Helicopter
came on the radio.

DANGER! TODAY'S STORM HAS KNOCKED LOOSE A BEAM ON THE NEW AXLEBURG HIGH-RISE! IT COULD FALL AT ANY MINUTE!
NEWS
3

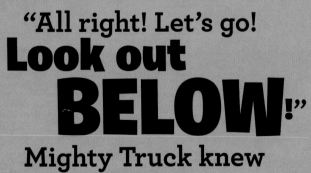

"All right! Let's go!
**Look out BELOW!**"
Mighty Truck knew
what he had to do.

"But how will I get somewhere so high in the air?" he wondered.

"Wait! *Air!* That's *it!*

"All right! Let's go!
**GROW, WHEELS, GROW!**"
Mighty Truck *pump*-pump-PUMPED air into
his tires . . .

PARK ↓

down onto another building . . .

WAY,

and **way,**

**BOING!**

**WAY** back up high— right on top of the high-rise!

Mighty Truck swept the dangling beam away from the edge of the roof . . . fired up his brightest headlights . . . and welded the loose girder back into place.

POOF!

Axleburg cheered as Mighty Truck
bounced safely onto a pile of dirt.
Everyone rushed to meet their new hero.
But all they found was grimy old Clarence.

"Did you see that through your filthy windshield?" Hattie asked. "Mighty Truck saved the day!"

Clarence considered telling her that *he* was Mighty Truck. But if anyone knew, they might expect him to stay clean all the time. And he really... really *wheely*... WHEELY really did not want that.

Not when getting dirty meant having fun.
"Besides," Clarence thought as he and Bruno finally
got those donuts, "help is only a wash away."